Spookball Champions

Written and illustrated by

Scoular Anderson

To Megan and Emma

Reprinted 2007, 2009
First paperback edition 2006
First published 2005 by
A & C Black Publishers Ltd
36 Soho Square, London, W1D 3QY

www.acblack.com

ISBN 978-0-7136-7253-4

A CIP catalogue for this book is available from the British Library.

This book is produced using paper that is made from wood grown in
managed, sustainable forests. It is natural, renewable and recyclable.
The logging and manufacturing processes conform to the
environmental regulations of the country of origin.

Printed and bound in Singapore by Tien Wah Press (Pte) Ltd

Chapter One

Oliver's mum and dad were away for the weekend, so he was staying with Aunty Mona and Uncle Fred.

They lived in a big, old house on top of a hill. Oliver was sure it was haunted.

Aunty Mona and Uncle Fred were very dull. They had no children, no neighbours, no cats and no dogs.

Aunty Mona moaned a lot.

Uncle Fred was very thin, so *he* didn't eat all the food. He just fretted a lot.

Oliver knew what was causing their problems.

Aunty Mona and Uncle Fred thought Oliver was being silly.

After dinner, Oliver was allowed to watch a programme on TV with the sound turned down.

The programme was about some people who lived in a big house by the sea. They turned it into a Bed and Breakfast.

That gave Oliver an idea.

Stop going on about ghosts, Oliver!!
It's time for bed.
We always go to bed early because we don't sleep well.

Your uncle kicks me in his sleep.
Your aunty pokes me in her sleep.

Oliver couldn't get to sleep.
He waited for the ghost, but it didn't appear.

He jumped out of bed.

He opened his weekend bag.
He was going to go
on a ghost hunt.

Chapter Two

Oliver had brought along some books and his Gameboy, and the ghost suit he had worn at Hallowe'en. He pulled it on.

He crept out of his room and along the landing.

He went downstairs.

He went across the hall, then down some more stairs. He stopped at a door.

He got ready to scare the ghost.

He pulled open the door.

It wasn't the kitchen.
It was a very untidy cupboard.

Oliver pushed all the stuff back.

He opened the next door. This *was* the kitchen and there was a ghost – a fat ghost munching her way through a packet of biscuits.

The ghost threw a biscuit at Oliver.

Oliver ducked and ran back upstairs.

He burst into Aunty and Uncle's bedroom and got another surprise. No wonder they didn't sleep well. There was a thin ghost lying between them.

At that moment, Aunty Mona woke up.
The thin ghost disappeared.

Oliver pulled his ghost hat off.

Aunty and Uncle were crosser than they had been before.

Chapter Three

Next day, Aunty Mona went to the supermarket, as usual.

Uncle Fred fretted about the squeaking doors and spent all day oiling the hinges.

Oliver just waited for bedtime.
He wanted to go on another ghost hunt.

That night, Oliver waited until the house was quiet, then he got up. He pulled on his ghost suit again.

He went upstairs this time. He climbed right to the top of the house.

The last stairs were very narrow and led to the attic. Slowly, he opened the attic door. Sure enough, there was a ghost.

Septimus told Oliver why he didn't like them.

Oliver felt sorry
for Septimus.

He didn't reach the other ghosts, though. He met Aunty Mona on the landing.

Chapter Four

Oliver had just got back into bed when he saw something move near the door. It was Septimus.

What happened?
Another ghost has arrived. He's challenged me to a game of spookball.
Can't you play?
I've lost my spooksticks.
What does a spookstick look like?
Come with me...

Septimus took Oliver back up to the top of the house. Quietly, they opened the attic door.

Caesar was tossing his spookstick from hand to hand.

Just then, Oliver remembered he had seen something like that before.

He ran back downstairs. He pulled open the cupboard next to the kitchen. All the stuff fell out again.

They were difficult to catch and hold because they were a bit like ghosts.

Before Oliver went back to the attic, he popped his head round the kitchen door.

He peeped into Aunty and Uncle's bedroom.

He reached the attic again.

Septimus didn't look keen.

Septimus took a spookstick and crept into the attic. The game of spookball was about to begin.

Chapter Five

All at once, a spookball flew across the attic. Caesar gave it a whack with his spookstick.

The ball zoomed down the attic and disappeared through the wall behind Septimus.

Caesar scored two more goals.

Another ball appeared. Septimus was quicker this time. He hit it through the wall behind Caesar Snarl.

Just then, something made Oliver turn round.

Horatio and Serina were coming up the stairs. They were holding spooksticks.

Horatio and Serina drifted past Oliver and up into the attic.

Oliver ran to his bedroom and pulled on his ghost suit. He went back upstairs and found the spare spookstick.

The spookballs were very fast.

Oliver soon got the hang of it.

The house shook
for a whole hour.
Windows rattled.
CREAK!
BLAM!
Doors
slammed.
WHOOSH!
GROAN!

Curtains billowed.

Lights flickered on and off.

Then the spookballs stopped coming. Sleepy Horatio had collapsed in a chair. Serina was slumped in a corner. She had eaten too many biscuits.

Just as Septimus whacked a ball past Caesar, the clock down in the hall struck midnight.

Caesar, Horatio and Serina were horrified.

A moment later, Caesar, Horatio and Serina vanished. Oliver saw them through a window, drifting off down the hill. The house belonged to Septimus once more.

Chapter Six

Next morning, Oliver got a surprise. Aunty and Uncle were smiling.

Uncle had got up early and made a sign.

Of course, Oliver knew better than that…

Oliver's mum and dad came to pick him up. Oliver promised to visit again soon. He was looking forward to another game of spookball in the attic.